The Tricky Trail

adapted by Maggie Testa
based on the screenplay "Mike the Knight and the
Tricky Trail" written by Gerard Foster

Ready-to-Read

Simon Spotlight
New York London Toronto Sydney New Delhi

SIMON SPOTLIGHT

An imprint of Simon & Schuster Children's Publishing Division

1230 Avenue of the Americas, New York, New York 10020

For information about special discounts for bulk purchases, please contact Simon & Schuster
Special Sales at 1-866-506-1949 or business@simonandschuster.com.

The Simon & Schuster Speakers Bureau can bring authors to your live event. For more information
or to book an event contact the Simon & Schuster Speakers Bureau at 1-866-248-3049 or visit our
website at www.simonspeakers.com.

Manufactured in the United States of America 0314 LAK

First Edition

10 9 8 7 6 5 4 3 2 1

ISBN 978-1-4424-9544-9 (pbk)

ISBN 978-1-4424-9545-6 (hc)

ISBN 978-1-4424-9546-3 (eBook)

Queen Martha has a special mission for Mike today. His sister, Evie, forgot her lunch. Can Mike bring it to her?

Mike will use his knightly tracking skills to find Evie.

Mike and his dragons look

for clues.

Sparkie does not see
any clues.

He sees flowers.

Flowers make him sneeze.

Then Sparkie sees a
shiny stone.
"It is just a stone,
not a clue," says Mike.

Mike sees footprints.

Footprints are clues.

Mike follows the footprints.

But the footprints do not
lead to Evie.

They lead to Trollee!

Mike sees broken twigs.

Twigs are clues.

"Evie must have stepped on them," says Mike.

But the twigs do not
lead to Evie.

They lead to a mud pit!

Sparkie shows Mike all the shiny stones he found.

They look like magic stones.

Evie must have left them.

The shiny stones are clues!

Mike follows the trail

of stones.

There is Evie!

She has a flower
for her sneezing spell.

The flower makes

Sparkie sneeze.

Sparkie blows fire when

he sneezes.

The flower is ruined.

Mike gives Evie her lunch.

But Evie does not want it.

She wants another flower.

Mike knows what to do. They saw the same flowers on their way to find Evie. They have to go back the way they came.

Mike will follow the trail.

Mike sees muddy

horseshoe prints.

Galahad made those prints.

"This way!" says Mike.

Mike follows the trail

past Trollee . . .

. . . all the way back

to the flower patch!

"We made it!" says Mike.

Huzzah!